T0131981

The Adventures of
Princeton & Ava-Paisley

Are We Ready For Bed?

Written & Illustrated by
♪ **Cynthia Marshall** ♪

To order additional copies of this book, contact:
Xlibris
844-714-8691
www.Xlibris.com
Orders@Xlibris.com

ISBN: 978-1-6641-7718-5 (sc)
ISBN: 978-1-6641-7717-8 (e)

Print information available on the last page

Rev. date: 05/27/2021

The Adventures of
Princeton & Ava-Paisley
Are We Ready For Bed?

Princeton and Ava have not been doing well going to bed together. They have not been going to bed at their normal bedtime.

They have been waking up extra tired in the morning because of staying up late while their mom is sleeping.

Sleeping in late has become a routine for them this week.

You guys can wake up now. You have been sleeping in lately. Are you guys ok? Asked, Mommy

Yes we are ok, said Ava

Ok lets get the day started.

Today we are going to clean your room.

You guys can help each other pick up all of your toys and I will do the rest.

Princeton and Ava didn't seem to happy about cleaning. They were still tired and wanted to sleep.

You guys have been yawning all morning. Let me help you guys pick up your toys.

While helping Princeton and Ava pick up toys, something fell out of one of the toys.

It looks like cookies that someone tried to hide. And also some candy.

You guys are not supposed to be taking snacks to your room. When did this happen?

At bedtime. Said, Ava

Princeton didn't want Ava to say anything. It was supposed to be their secret.

When its bedtime you have to get your rest.

Said, Mommy

Princeton and Ava finished cleaning their room. While cleaning their room they promised each other to go to bed when they are supposed to.

We have to really go to bed and not pretend anymore. Said, Princeton

We can turn the tv off after we brush our teeth. That will help us sleep faster.

Princeton and Ava spent the rest of the day thinking of ways to help with their bedtime. Before they knew it, it was almost time for bed.

It's almost bedtime guys. Let's get ready. Said, Mommy

We decided to turn the tv off tonight that way we can be ready for bedtime.

Not only did Princeton and Ava turn the tv off, but they took their covers and tucked themselves into bed to have a good night sleep.

Let's say our prayers before you guys fall asleep.

After a few minutes of laying down Princeton and Ava were sleeping. They slept all night with their excitement of being ready for bedtime.

The next morning came. Princeton and Ava were up early.

Good morning guys, how was bedtime?

It was great. Said, Princeton

I'm glad you guys learned that having a bedtime and proper sleep is good for you. I am so proud of you both.

What do you do before going to bed?

Printed in the United States
by Baker & Taylor Publisher Services